Paste your photo here!

This book is dedicated to
Jack, Preston, and Josephine.

ISBN 978-0-8118-7148-8

Manufactured by Main Choice, Dong Guan City, China, in May 2010.

1 3 5 7 9 10 8 6 4 2

This product conforms to CPSIA 2008.

Chronicle Books LLC
680 Second Street, San Francisco, California 94107

www.chroniclekids.com

ALL ABOUT ME,

MY WORLD, AND MY LIFE (SO FAR)

By _____

Write your name here

chronicle books · san francisco

THE BASICS

Julius and the gang want to get to know you!

I am a . . .

☐ Boy   ☐ Girl

I am _____ years old.

My birthday is on _____.

I am _____ tall.
(measurement)

What color are your eyes? Circle the color.

Is your hair curly, wavy, or straight? Circle one.

curly

wavy

straight

What color is your hair exactly? Draw an arrow pointing to the color.

PORTRAITS OF ME

A picture is worth a thousand words! Make your portrait!

My face

My whole
self

My profile

My foot
(wearing my favorite shoe)

MY HAND & FOOT

Trace your hand and foot so you can come back to this book next year to see how much they've grown!

Trace your hand here:

This is how big my hand was on:

_____
(date)

Trace your foot here:

**This is how big
my foot was on:**

_____
(date)

MY FAMILY

Let's get to know your family.

There are _____ people in my family, and _____ pets.

I have _____ brothers and _____ sisters.

Here are the names of everyone in my family:

_____

_____

_____

This is my favorite thing to do with my family:

_____

_____

_____

_____

Draw a family portrait.

My family

THINGS I CAN DO

Everybody has things they can do well.
What about you?

Can you . . . draw skate

ride a horse bake cupcakes write stories

do a headstand swim

paint ride a bike (Circle the ones you can do.)

I'm a spectacular DJ!

What else can you do? Make a list here!

I bet there are a few other things that you do that your friends and family would say are RAD! Ask a bunch of them to write (or draw!) something special that you do.

X Signed by: _____ Date: _____

X Signed by: _____ Date: _____

X Signed by: _____ Date: _____

X Signed by: _____ Date: _____

MY HOME

I live in a . . .

(Circle one.)

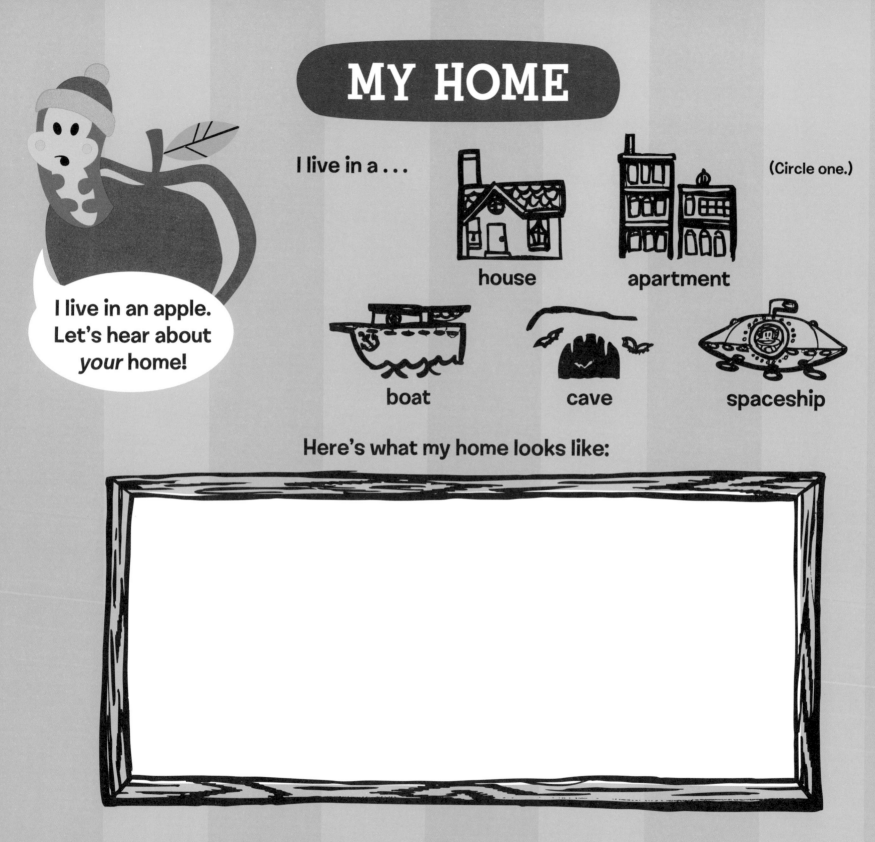

house

apartment

boat

cave

spaceship

I live in an apple. Let's hear about *your* home!

Here's what my home looks like:

The best place to hide for hide-and-seek in my house is _____.

Here's a picture of my room:

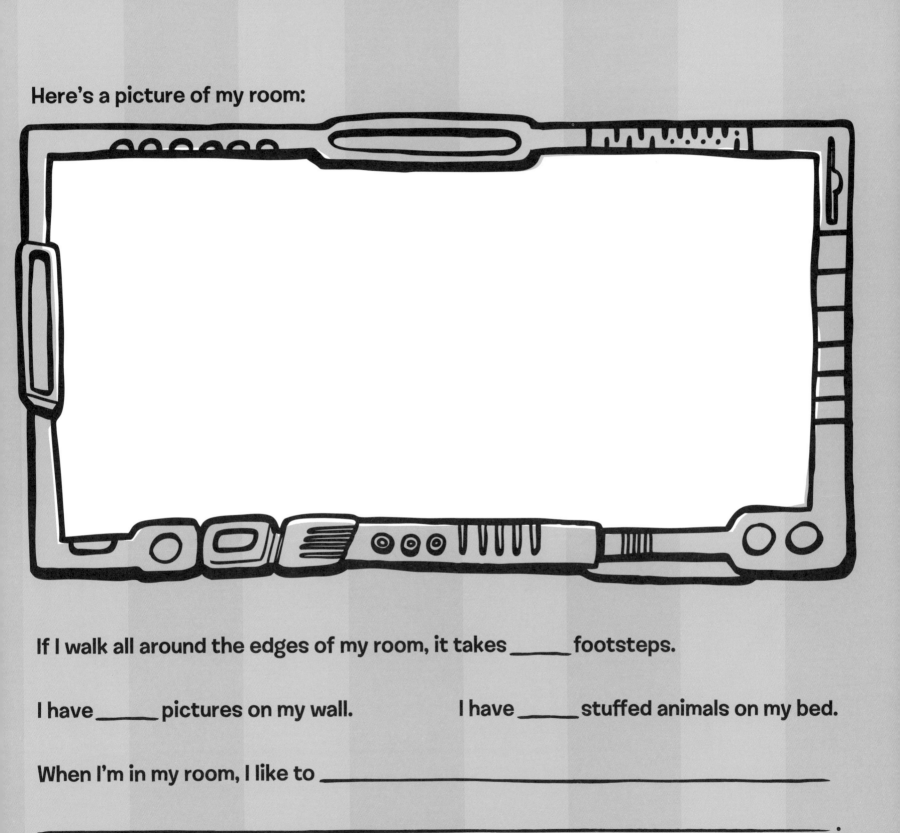

If I walk all around the edges of my room, it takes _____ footsteps.

I have _____ pictures on my wall.   I have _____ stuffed animals on my bed.

When I'm in my room, I like to _____

_____.

MY SCHOOL

My school is called _____.

I get to school by: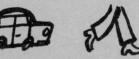

(Circle one.)

My favorite class in school is art. What's *your* favorite class?

This is a map of how I get there:

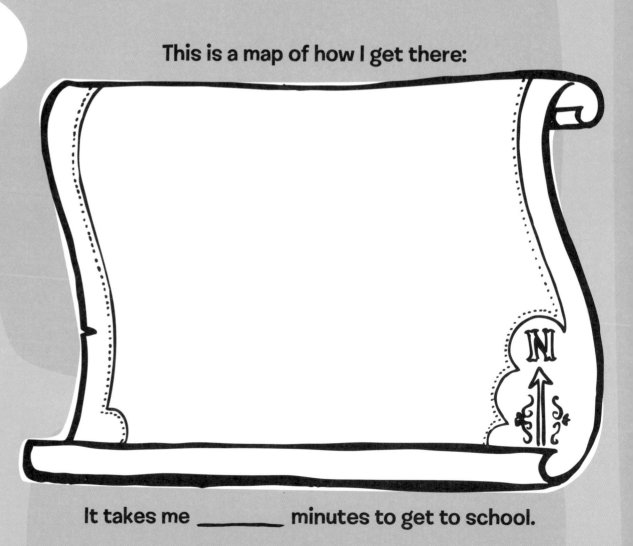

It takes me _____ minutes to get to school.

These are all the subjects
I study at school:

_____

_____

_____

_____

_____

Here is a picture of a teacher I like:

Write the teacher's name here:

Aa Bb Cc Dd Ee Ff Gg Hh Ii J

The people I have the most fun with are _____ .

My favorite class is _____ .

Here are some things I learned at school this year: _____

_____

_____

STUFF I DO AFTER SCHOOL

After school, I like to do these things: _____

_____

_____

I spend time with: _____

Here's a picture of my favorite
after-school snack:

BOOKS & SHOWS I LOVE

My favorite books are:

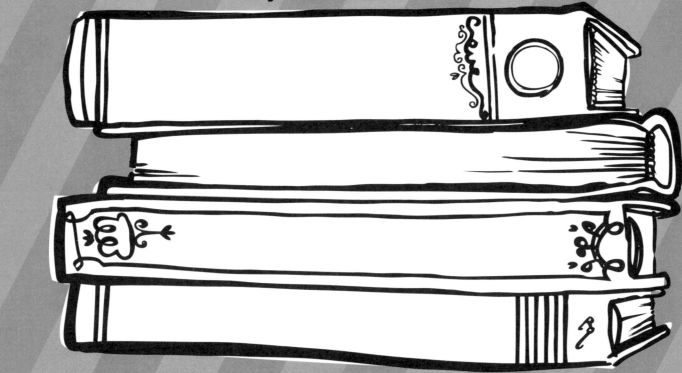

Here's a picture of my favorite show:

I also like to watch these shows:

_____

_____

_____

_____

MY FAVORITE FOODS

Here's my favorite food of all:

_____

My favorite vegetable

My favorite drink:

My favorite fruit

My favorite ice cream flavor:

My favorite pizza topping:

My favorite dessert:

Oh, and I **don't like** to eat _____ .

MY FAVORITE MUSIC

The last song I listened to was _____.

Here are my favorite songs:

_____

_____

_____

_____

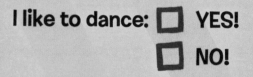

I like to dance: ☐ YES!
                        ☐ NO!

I like to sing: ☐ YES!
                      ☐ NO!

THE CLOTHES I WEAR...AND DON'T!

My favorite outfit of all

My favorite pajamas

My favorite socks

My favorite T-shirt

Oh, and **please** don't make me wear _____.

A STORY BY ME!

Tell a story about something you did that was really fun. Who was with you? What was the best part?

_____

_____

_____

_____

_____

_____

_____

_____

SPORTS & GAMES I LIKE

My favorite sport to play is _____.

My favorite sport to watch is _____.

These are my favorite games to play: _____
_____

Here's a picture of me playing my favorite sport or game:

PLACES I'VE BEEN... AND WANT TO GO!

Here are the places I have been so far:

_____

_____

_____

_____

_____

The farthest away I have ever gone is to _____.

My favorite place to travel is to _____.

I **really** want to go to _____

_____.

A FEW OF MY FAVORITES...

What's your favorite color?
Draw an arrow pointing to it.

Wait . . . there are
a few more things we
want to find out!

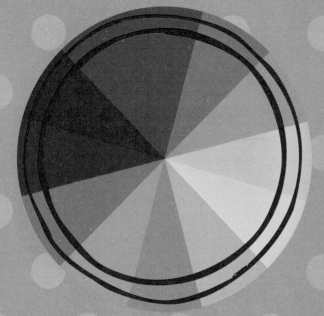

My favorite animal: _____

My favorite smell: _____

My favorite weather: _____

My favorite games or toys: _____

My favorite time of day: _____

My favorite thing about morning: _____

My favorite thing about nighttime: _____

...AND NOT-FAVORITES

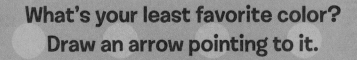

What's your least favorite color?
Draw an arrow pointing to it.

My least favorite animal: _____

My least favorite smell: _____

My least favorite weather: _____

My least favorite games or toys: _____

My least favorite time of day: _____

My least favorite thing about morning: _____

My least favorite thing about nighttime: _____

WHEN I GROW UP

When I grow up, I want to be a _____.

When I grow up, I'm going to live in a _____
and travel to work by _____.

Here's a picture of my future house:

Here's a picture of me, all grown up:

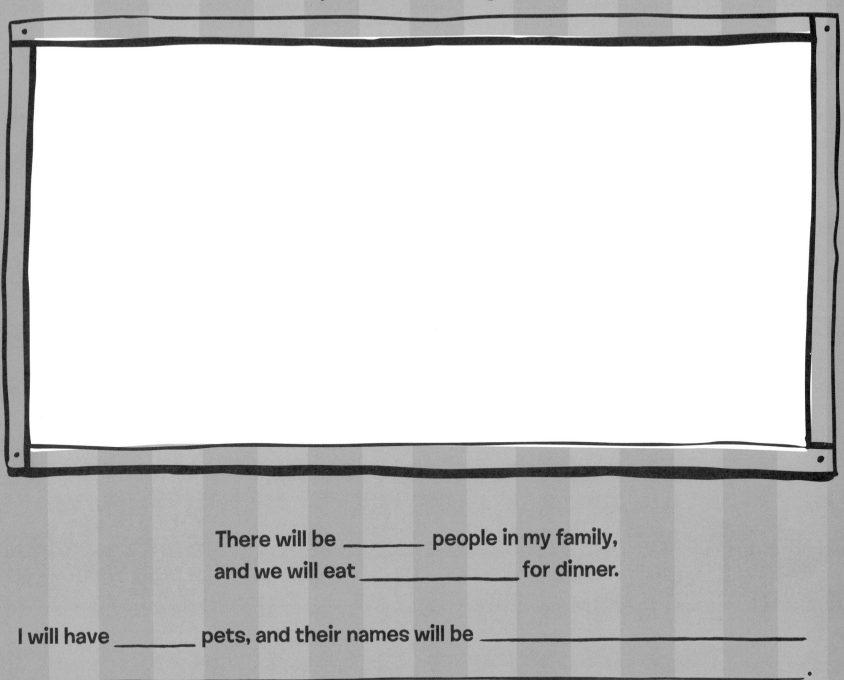

There will be _____ people in my family,
and we will eat _____ for dinner.

I will have _____ pets, and their names will be _____
_____.